Plastic Planet

T0337562

Contents

Written by Charlotte Guillain

Collins

What is plastic?

Look around and you will probably see plastic everywhere. We use plastic to make chairs, food wrappers, fabric and many other things!

Plastic is made using oil, gas or coal.
Scientists discovered how to make the first plastics in the nineteenth century.

Why do we use plastic?

Plastic is waterproof, **flexible** and cheap to make. Its appearance can differ. It can be colourful or clear. Some plastics are thick and strong, and some are thin and light.

People like plastic because it is easy to clean and it can be made into any shape. So what is wrong with plastic?

What is wrong with plastic?

Plastic seems like a great invention but it can't **break down**. This means it can't rot away over time. It stays around for centuries.

Plastic rubbish gets blown into water, such as rivers.
Then it gets washed into the sea.

When sea animals find plastic, they can mistake it for food. Seals think plastic wrappers are jellyfish and can swallow them.

Other creatures climb into packaging or get stuck in plastic wrapping and can't wriggle free. Turtles can get caught in fishing nets.

Plastic rubbish is carried on the sea's **currents** and can move all around the world. It cannot break down so it can remain in the sea for many years.

Today there are huge patches of plastic rubbish floating in the sea, bringing destruction to the wildlife there. Sea animals need our protection.

11

What action can people take?

Some plastic can be recycled and made into something new. Most people know they need to put plastic wrappers in their recycling bin.

However, not all plastic can be recycled. Also, it takes **energy** to recycle plastic. It would be better not to have the plastic in the first place.

It's a great idea to reuse things made of plastic. Ask an adult to cut the bottom off plastic containers with scissors.
Then decorate them and fill them with plants or pencils!

Single-use plastic is used just once. You use it, then throw it away. You can take action by avoiding single-use plastic!

You can use this knowledge to help. Use as little plastic as possible. Don't use plastic straws. You can use a metal straw or go without instead.

Always carry a water bottle with you. Then you won't need new plastic bottles. This can help reduce the creation of new plastic bottles. There are many places to refill your bottle.

Make sure you take a backpack with you to the shops. Then you won't need to pay for a plastic bag to carry your shopping.

Help your parents pick food with no plastic wrapping. You could weigh loose apples instead of getting them in a plastic bag.

Try using shampoo bars!

Your mission!

Try to avoid using plastic as much as you can. This can be your mission to help our beautiful planet.

Glossary

break down rot away

current direction sea water flows

energy power, such as electricity

flexible bendy

Avoiding plastic

After reading

Letters and Sounds: Phases 5–6

Word count: 502

Focus phonemes: /n/ kn /m/ mb /r/ wr /s/ c, ce, sc /sh/ ti, ssi, s

Common exception words: of, to, the, into, are, do, once, our, their, people, today, because, great, break, beautiful, water, many, any, move, parents

Curriculum links: Science: Everyday materials

National Curriculum learning objectives: Reading/word reading: apply phonic knowledge and skills as the route to decode words, read common exception words, noting unusual correspondences between spelling and sound and where these occur in the word; read other words of more than one syllable that contain taught GPCs; Reading/comprehension: develop pleasure in reading, motivation to read, vocabulary and understanding by being encouraged to link what they read or hear to their own experiences

Developing fluency

- Your child may enjoy hearing you read the book.
- Take turns to read a page of the main text, pausing at commas and between sentences.

Phonic practice

- Focus on words with more than one syllable and /s/ and /sh/ sounds.
- Challenge your child to read the following, breaking the words into sounds and syllables if necessary to help them.

  re-cy-cled   pro-tec-tion   app-ear-ance   mi-ssion

- Take turns to choose a multisyllabic word for the other to read. Challenge your child to identify any /s/ or /sh/ sounds.

Extending vocabulary

- Look at the glossary on page 21. Discuss other words that could be in this glossary. Challenge your child to decide on a definition for each word.

Comprehension

- Turn to pages 22 and 23. Discuss what each item is made from. If it is plastic, is it single-use or can it be re-used?